Hellspawn and Other Stories
Femdom Mind Control
Flash Fiction – Vol. 39

S.B.

Disclaimer

This is a work of fiction. Names, characters, business, events, and incidents are the products of the author's imagination. Any resemblance to actual persons, living or dead, or actual events is purely coincidental. All characters are over 18.

Table of Contents

One hell of a time is waiting for you.

A special "thank you" to

all patrons of Spell... B-O-U-N-D.

Find the Man

Otto squinted as he stared into the tablet's screen for the umpteenth time and saw absolutely nothing except a mishmash of shapes with no sense of order to them. This was getting ridiculous, and not in a good way!

The puzzles had started out easy enough. All he had to do was find a specific animal in each of the pictures presented to him and circle it out. A lonely panda in a sea of penguins? Easy! An orange cat pressed against a carpet of the same color? Please! If the goal was to stump him, they would have to do a lot better than that, and so they did.

The third image was way trickier than the ones that came before. Another second and he would have missed the spider on the sand, much to his chagrin. However, the fourth was utter and complete bullshit. The timer ran its natural course, and he grumbled when the answer was presented to him.

"Oh, come on! That's not fair," he said.

"What's wrong?" Dr. Elizabeth Riker, the woman in charge of the visual study, asked.

"That's not a bear in the picture, but some branches photoshopped to appear like the outline of one."

"What's the difference, Otto?"

"Well, duh! One is a real beast, and the other is a fabrication. This was a trick question!"

"And the first one wasn't?"

"Huh?"

"The panda was added digitally to the picture too, or do you often see them hanging out with their penguin friends in Antarctica?"

"That's not the same thing."

"Of course, it is. This is all about perception, and sometimes that means thinking outside the box. What you see isn't always what you get. You can't be too literal with these things just like you can't be too literal when moving through life."

"Please spare me the philosophical mumbo-jumbo. That's not what I signed up for!"

"Oh, I know, but you won't get a cent until you complete the whole set, so how about we continue?"

"Fine!"

Otto held the tablet close to his reading glasses and looked at the new picture. The snake was almost perfectly camouflaged against the tree bark, but he noticed it right away. The dog's shadow reflected on the wall that came afterward didn't give him any grievances either. He was on a roll again and this time nothing would stop him from collecting the prize money at the...

"Fuck! Are you for real now?"

"What is it this time?" Dr. Riker smirked.

"What nonsense is this? I don't understand what you want me to do."

"What's not to understand? All you need to do is find the man."

"Yeah, about that..."

The picture comprised a mass of kneeling individuals by an altar where a radiant goddess shone in all her splendor. The center of the image was the only thing that remained static with everything else undulating all around.

"What are you trying to say?"

"There are hundreds of men in this picture!"

"Are you sure?"

"Yes, I'm sure. There are at least ten in this row, ten above it, ten more here..."

"Look closely."

Otto blinked, peering into the depths of the 2D representation. The human figures were still there in plain view but so were the small oddities he hadn't noticed at first glance... the shackles around their arms and legs... tight leather collars around their necks... the supplicant poses that were never addressed... so many details blending into one another as the colors rippled and phased in and out of his mind.

Dr. Riker stopped in front of him and pointed at the floor.

"Can you find the man now?" she asked.

"No."

"Why not?"

"They're all slaves."

"Now that's the proper way of thinking... Shall we move on to the next picture?"

"I think I'd rather stare at this one a while longer..." he mumbled, his vision beginning to decline alongside his thoughts.

"Yes, I suspected as much. Take your time and when you're ready we can discuss how useful you'll become to me."

Otto nodded. He had already found what he never knew he wanted until that day. The money already forgotten, he sank deeper into the good doctor's control.

Game-Changer

To say that Marsha was uncomfortable sitting across from her mother in a fancy Manhattan restaurant was an understatement. There were two main reasons for that with the first being she hated needless extravaganza and the second that she hadn't seen her progenitor in a decade. She would have been happy for that to continue, but alas! that was not to be.

Diane, the sexagenarian who had been a swimsuit model in a previous life, was all gold that night from the dress to the shoes, the bracelets around her wrists, and even her eyes. Colorful contacts had never looked good on her, but she didn't care. From the moment she had learned to speak her mind, Diane had always done things her way regardless of who she had to hurt to make them happen.

The waiting game for the meal was atrocious and so was the promise of small talk. Marsha wanted out and didn't take long to say it out loud.

"Why are we here again?" she asked, sipping a ginger ale.

"Can't a mother spend some quality time with her only daughter?" Diane retorted.

"You lost that right the last time we were together, or have you forgotten what you said and did?"

"I haven't, but it's been so long. Why haven't you forgiven me for that yet?"

"Because telling me I should burn in hell for 'daring to be a lesbian' is not something you forgive that easily, mother!" Marsha spat.

"I was wrong, okay? I've turned a new page ever since and now I'm happier than ever. I wanted you here to share that happiness with you. Will you at least give me a chance?"

"Make it quick then."

"I will. Just waiting for... ah, here he comes! Get ready to be amazed."

Indeed, she was. Seeing her mother after so much time was already surprising, but her estranged father too? And they were kissing? Huh?

"Hello, honey. It's nice to see you," Richard said.

"Dad? What are you...? Wait, are you two together again?"

"We are, but not in the way you think," Diane smirked.

"What's that supposed to mean?"

"I'll just have to show you," Diane flashed a golden ring with a single black gem engraved in its center. "Sit down, slave."

"Yes, Goddess," Richard replied, his eyes going blank. Whatever life there had been in them was now buried under a veil of complete mindlessness. When Marsha looked at him, she no longer saw a man but a flesh puppet making a terrible impression at being one.

"Surprise!" Diane exclaimed. "What do you think?"

"I don't understand what just happened," Marsha frowned. "Is Dad okay?"

"He's great. Your father was never a good man, but that's all in the past now. It's amazing what a little hypnotic conditioning can do."

"Hypnosis? Seriously?"

"Yep. Some intensive training, good old triggers, and something for him to focus on and suddenly all problems are easily fixed. He sucked as a husband, but he can only grow better as a servant. Isn't this something else?"

"If you say so..."

"You don't seem too excited."

"I'm sorry, was I supposed to be?"

"Well, yes. Think about this can change your life too. If I could turn your father into a pet, I can do the same to everyone else. This changes everything and I want you to be a part of that change, too."

"You've got to be kidding me! So, your solution to life's problems from now is to make them go away with hypnosis? Do you even realize how ridiculous that sounds?"

"You'll think differently once you learn your place. I promise you the first time you see someone drop for you will be something you'll want to repeat over and over."

"And why are you so certain about that?"

"Lesbian or not, you're still my daughter. I know what blood runs in your veins. Forget what I said about hell, okay? Let me give you a slice of Heaven."

"Not happening, Mother. God, I feel so stupid right now!" Marsha laid down the empty glass on the table and said, "I'm leaving."

"Are you sure?" Diane tapped the base of the glass, forcing her eyes to look at it. Traces of a white powder remained at the bottom. "I'm sorry, but this is for your own good, dear."

"You... you drugged me?"

"No. He did, Marsha," she pointed at the waiter that was arriving with their food. "I told you hypnosis is a game-changer, didn't I? You did well, slave."

"Thank you, Mistress," he said. "Enjoy your meal."

"I'll enjoy everything, I'm sure. And you too, Marsha. This will be fun."

Feeling her conscious self slowly slipping away from her, the young woman's jaw went slack.

Hellspawn

Xavier entered his boss's office precisely one minute before the end of his shift. Being summoned so late in the day, especially on a Friday, was never a good sign. He was about to be fucked again.

Tiffany Winters saw him standing by the door and snapped her fingers. "What are you waiting for? Come here!"

"What can I do for you, Miss Winters?" he asked, hands behind his back. Anyone fluent in body posture could tell he was doing his best to contain his seething anger, yet his best would never be enough.

"I'm having a party tomorrow night in my place and one of the staff just called in sick. Since you've got nothing better to do anyway, I need you to cover for him," she handed him a black and red card with embroidered golden letters. "Here's the address. The party starts at eight, but you are required to be there two hours earlier at least to help with the last preparations. Are we clear? Good."

"I'm sorry, is this a joke?" he clenched his fists.

"No. Why would it be? Do you have a problem with what I just told you to do?"

"I do. My contract ties me to your company, not your private life, Miss Winters. I don't have any obligation to work for you outside these premises and I find your presumptions about how I spend my free time rather insulting." he threw the card back at her much to the surprise of the young multi-millionaire.

"I see..." she yawned disdainfully. "Is there anything you'd like to add?"

"Only that I'm leaving for the weekend and that there's no way I'll be serving at your party tomorrow or any other day. Goodbye."

"Not so fast!" she snapped her fingers again producing a copy of his contract written in what appeared to be an ancient gold parchment. Black fingernails pointed at one of the bottom sections. "Correct me if I'm wrong but doesn't it clearly state here that your workplace is determined by me alone and that your functions can change depending on my personal needs?"

"I... hmm... what? Since when has that clause been there?"

"Since always, of course. Work relations are treated seriously in this company, and I would do nothing to abuse my (superior) position, of course. Now, right at the bottom, do you mind reading what's written there?"

"I'd rather not..."

"Too bad because that's an order. What does it say, Xavier?"

"Any attempt of refusal or disobedience to a direct command may be met with severe punishment, the harshest of them all being the obliteration of one's immortal soul..." he read, a veil of darkness enveloping both the office and his mind.

"That's right, and that's your signature in blood at the end, is it not?"

"I guess, but..."

"Spare me the excuses, Xavier. I don't want to punish you, but I will if you don't get your shit together. You will obey, won't you?" she growled.

"Yes, Miss Winters. Whatever you say."

"Good. And so you don't forget who's in charge, be there right after lunch instead of arriving at six. I'll keep you busy until the festivities begin."

"Yes, Miss Winters."

"Dismissed!"

Xavier left the office, head hanging low. She was such a bitch, but it came with the territory. He should have known she would play the "starving demon" card on him.

Tiffany smirked as he almost soiled himself on his way out, utterly convinced of her supernatural nature. No one under her command loved her and "Hellspawn" was one of the most common insults whispered in the corridors when referring to her. What better way to capitalize on that than with some good old mental rewiring? Every computer in the company automatically ran a subliminal program when turned on, and the messages that were pushed into their subconscious minds reinforced the illusion of her demonic persona. Fear was the ultimate motivator and the best way to grow an army of slaves for her every need. She knew that now and the results couldn't be better.

She glanced at a list of names and called the next one. There were other positions in need of free labor.

Just Wait and See

Susan Hayes was the typical sorority girl you often see in movies and TV shows, a young big-breasted blonde with a tremendous desire to be popular but somehow never quite made the cut and found herself often resenting the unfairness of it all as if her life began and ended at twenty. Her personality was inconstant yet possessed one markedly deciding trait. She hated being told what she could or couldn't do.

So, on the day she found out that her "sisters" were planning a party behind her back, a gathering for which they had no intention of inviting her despite sharing a dorm together, she felt angry and betrayed and demanded an explanation,

"What gives, Olivia? Why am I being kept out of the loop on this one?"

"Oh, it's a hypnotic party," Olivia Barrington, the only daughter of TV tycoon Richard Barrington, replied. "We know you're not into hypnosis and this is something you would never agree with, so..."

"What? No! Who told you something like that? I love hypnosis!"

"Do you really?" Janice Peters asked. She was a lovely African American with the body of a Goddess that was being coveted by modeling agencies around the world for a while now. Her ironic smiles were the best in business, and she had just used one on her to make a point.

"Yeah, and I don't think it's fair for you to do this without me. I want in. When's the party?"

"Next Saturday, at 10 pm, but are you sure you can handle it?" Olivia asked.

"Positive. I'll be there."

"Okay."

The week went by in a flash, almost as if all of Time was eager for what was about to happen. Susan was one of the first to arrive, but the games were already underway when she did. The first thing she saw when entering the adjacent pavilion to the sorority house was Miss "Goody-Two-Shoes" Linda Walker helplessly staring at a swinging pocket watch.

"What's going on?" Susan approached Olivia, a glass of fruit punch in her right hand.

"Oh, she's always so stiff that we thought of relaxing her a bit before we got started. Linda has a secret, you know?"

"What secret?"

"She turns into quite a slut when she's under, not that such a thing would ever happen to you."

"What do you mean?"

"Come on, Susan! You just wanted to be here to not feel left out. I doubt you can even enter trance let alone let your wild side come out and play! Face it, girl. That's just not you, but hey, you insisted on coming..."

"Excuse me?" Susan lashed out, barely resisting the temptation of smashing the glass on the floor. "That's a fucking lie! I can have as much fun as everyone else if not more and if Linda can be entranced, then why can't I? I bet I'm a wonderful subject deep inside and I sure as hell can be the biggest slut of them all."

"So nice to hear you say that," Janice whispered in her right ear. "Hold on to that thought for me."

A silver pendant appeared before the infuriated young woman's eyes, swinging back and forth, back and forth, inviting her to let go, give in, and enjoy her drop into mesmerizing seduction. Nobody told her what was off-limits! Nobody! She would show them her real self, the horny bitch lying dormant since the first day at college. Yes, she would definitely... show... them...

"Sleep, Susan," Janice commanded, wrapping the chain of the pendant around her neck as she complied. "Deeper now, powerless to resist. As long as this is pressed against your body, you will obey us. Obey, Susan. It's what you want."

Susan Hayes was the sluttiest girl on campus. She loved to ram 7-inch ice dildos down her throat and lick the soles of their beautiful owners while they filmed it all for future reference. At one point, she remembered them saying it was a shame she couldn't become a full-fledged porn star to entertain them throughout the rest of the year.

"Says who?" she muttered, going even deeper. "Just wait and see."

Magic is Real

Kate dusted the top half of her wardrobe and stared in awe at something she hadn't seen in ages. The small box with a wood carving of a flower bouquet on the lid was a treasure trove of memories of a shared distant past with Jenna. She picked it up, descended from the small set of stairs, and sat on the bed to examine it.

Inside, there were colorful pictures of their first dates; movie stubs that reminded her of the days when everything wasn't digital and available on-demand at the press of a button; a collection of handwritten poems that, while not very good, were at least meaningful enough to make her shed a tear; and the most arresting object of all, one she had dreamed about for many years after their story had ended. It was Jenna's favorite ring, a silver coiled beauty she has always said to possess magical powers.

"There's no such thing as magic," Kate had said the first time she heard the supernatural explanation.

"Of course, there is. It's all around us in everything you see. Magic binds the universe and the souls living in it. It's because of it we're here today."

"And I thought it was because of your cheeky smile and cute freckles, dear."

"This ring sensed you were the one for me and this ring is never wrong."

"Do you really believe that?"

"Yes."

Kate never did though she didn't mind playing along. Jenna was adorable in every sense of the word, and she loved her truly. Time was kind to them, yet it never stopped, just like a river and its endless flow. It continued long after her heart stopped beating and it was still doing it that day.

"You were one of a kind, my love," she said.

"We're all one-of-a-kind, Kate. What makes us 'us' is unique and unrepeatable. You will never have what you and I used to have..."

"I know."

"... but magic doesn't cease just because we stop looking for it. The ring is yours now, and you know what to do."

"I don't want to."

"So you think, but thoughts can be wrong. Your confusion will go away if you wear it."

Sacrilege! Blasphemy or worse! Unlike what other people thought, putting that ring on was the same as wearing her lover's corpse like a piece of clothing and while the memories were pleasant, the ghosts themselves were not.

"Just once, Kate, for once is enough. Will you do that for me?"

Kate sighed as she played with the box. She had never expected to see it again and yet now it would not go away even if she tried to forget it somewhere else. She put on the piece of jewelry and stepped out of the house, embracing the sun of a warm Spring day.

The first thing she saw was a moving truck parking by the entrance of the house next door and a charming redhead looking her way. Their eyes met for a second, and then she smiled. Kate's right hand glowed.

Yes, magic was real, and the ring was never wrong.

May These Words...

Let's talk about words. I promise this won't take long and that you'll not be bored by what you're about to read if you just approach things with an open mind. Can you do that for me? Good.

The thing I love most about words is not that we use them to simply communicate with one another, but also to imagine things. Even if we're having a hard time expressing ourselves, the proper combination of sounds can trigger the most unexpected results, so to talk about words also means to talk about imagination, so let's go there.

I would like you to imagine something for me. Imagine a beautiful woman dressed in whatever type of outfit makes you horny, whether it's a leather jacket, a latex skirt, or even some Yoga pants. Now picture her walking your way, stopping close enough to get your juices flowing, and then saying,

"Hello. I'm going to stupefy you."

It doesn't sound that great, right? It's not what most people would consider sexy at all, even though 'stupefy' is a great word. For instance, it's one of the possible synonyms of "hypnotize" and if you use this last word instead, suddenly the sentence above becomes something incredibly hot, to the point you'd probably lose your composure before even realizing what was happening to you. That's the power that comes with using the right words at the right times.

Context is always important and not only when you're trying to make a good impression. Without it, even the most elaborate speech of all is rendered perfectly meaningless.

Let's go back to the previous example. Imagine that same woman that already got under your skin with her sexy ways, placing a delicate finger under your chin, forcing you to stare into her majestic eyes, and then adding,

"This is how you'll be narcotized."

Be honest: how you would react in this situation? I think you'd be shocked, and the initial spell would break somehow and all because the words you were expecting to hear were simply not there. Sure, you could try to ignore it, but the little voice in your head would still probably say, "Damn it! Why did she have to ruin everything?"

Words are powerful tools for imagination indeed, but we often hold on to imagined words so dearly that we don't like the real ones that come our way and that's wrong, because life isn't perfect, and people aren't perfect. We don't always say the things we want to say in the way people expect us to, and the opposite is also true. We make mistakes, stumble and fall. Sometimes, it feels like our tongue is stuck, and our thoughts are stuck with it, and only after the perfect moment is gone, do we realize what we could have done differently. These things happen and they're usually not pretty, but they're genuine, and genuine things matter. Remember this always.

And now that this taste of reality has been read and hopefully assimilated, you deserve a treat, so imagine one last thing for me. The woman you can't stop thinking about has sat on your lap, grinding her ass against your groin. She wets her lips and gently pushes a strand of hair over her right ear. Suspended by her breathtaking beauty, you realize you're on the verge of something wonderful, and this time, it doesn't disappoint. She touches your forehead and says,

"You are my now obedient hypno-slave. Sleep!"

Hmmm... how perfect is that? Sweet dreams, pet, and may these words never leave your mind.

More, Please!

The hot wax dripped around Ashley's navel, sliding dangerously close to her shaved pussy. The young redhead arched her back atop the kitchen table and moaned,

"Hmmm, more."

"What did you say, slut?" Roxanne asked, holding the peppermint candle firmly in her right hand. Recent studies had hypothesized that the scent enhanced sexual desire in women and could help them achieve multiple orgasms, and by the looks of it they were right. Ashley, who was usually a quiet and deserved woman, could barely keep it together, pearls of sweat glistening on her naked body, and dark green eyes burning with ever-increasing lust.

"More, Mistress. Please... I need it!"

"So you say," the older blonde tilted the candle once more, this time over her right leg. "... but do you really deserve it?"

"I... I think so. I've been good, Mistress. You know that."

"How can you be good when you're still doing the one thing you're not supposed to do, slut?"

"Hmmm? What's that, Mistress?"

"Thinking..." Roxanne said, placing a wet finger on her lips. "I really don't like it when you do that."

"Oh, I..."

"Quiet, slut. If you really want to be rewarded, you need to listen first. Stare at the candle."

Ashley adjusted her body position to face the flickering flame, burning in mesmerizing shades of red, orange, and yellow. It was almost as captivating as her owner's eyes, and she already knew what was coming next.

"Repeat after me, I'm my Mistress's horny slut."

"I'm my Mistress's horny slut."

"Only her pleasure matters, not mine."

"Only her pleasure matters, not mine."

"It pleases her when I don't think at all."

"It pleases her when I don't think at all."

"Sluts don't need thoughts, only obedience."

"Sluts don't need thoughts, only obedience."

"I always obey my owner's commands."

"I always obey my owner's commands."

"Making her happy is the only reason I live for."

"Making her happy is the only reason I live for."

"I will sink into the flame and stop thinking right now."

"I will sink into the flame and stop thinking right now."

"Very good, slut. Sleep!"

Ashley's head gently fell on the table, arms and legs twitching into a bewildering stupor that made her completely powerless. Three drops of wax burned her right thigh.

Roxanne hopped on the table and slid her lace panties down, cunt against cunt, exchanging warm fluids of unbridled sex. She then placed the candle on her pet's belly button and said,

"Don't move or this will hurt."

There it stood like it were a birthday and Ashley the yummy cake everyone wanted a piece of, but only her got to eat it and enjoy. While Roxanne loved to play hard to content like any skilled, mischievous Domme, she recognized those that were good to her and there was no better than her entranced slut. Whether it was with a candle, an ice cube, a spatula, or any other unusual implement she could find, Ashley was always ready for her and as long as that wonderment remained, so would she. Gently caressing her favorite pet's perky breasts, Roxanne smiled as the candle died out.

Prelude

Dylan Mason considered himself to be a well-rounded man with his life perfectly controlled. He had a steady job, dependable friends, and actually loved spending Thanksgiving and Christmas with family. He didn't drink, didn't smoke, and had never tried drugs (not even recreational) in his life. A sports aficionado, he only had one secret addiction that was as honeyed as irresistible. He loved breakfast cereals. Not a single day went by when he didn't eat a bowl first thing in the morning usually accompanied with cold milk. The processed sugars and artificial flavors were a bit overkill, but he was always eager to try something new, so going to the supermarket on a weekend was always an adventure. What he would try next?

On that cold spring Saturday morning, he stood in his favorite aisle, looking at the colorful card boxes and the delicacies within. He had already spotted two new flavors from his favorite brand as well as some sprinkled UFOs that wanted to "beam him into a world of chocolate." The tagline was horrible, but he still wanted to try them. In his perfect contemplative pose, he was like a monk in trance, yet his cogitations were interrupted by the screeching sound of a shopping cart and the lovely woman pushing it.

She was an Asian American with long black hair and the warmest of smiles also on the hunt for something sweet. When her cart nearly bumped into the awkward and yet athletic man, anyone paying close attention could see the sparks flying almost instantly.

"Sorry," she said. "I wasn't paying much attention."

"It's my fault, really. I'm like a statue over here."

"Tough choice, huh?" she pointed at the shelves in front of them.

"You have no idea. They're all so good."

"Until you eat too much and get a stomachache..."

"Luckily, that never happens to me."

"That's good. Have you ever tried these?" She pointed at a black and blue box right on the edge of his field of vision.

"I don't think so. What's so special about them?"

"Oh, I like the way they're shaped most of all. Cute little spirals for hypnotic encounters..."

"Hypnotic, huh? Now, that's a first."

"There's always a first time for everything, isn't there?"

"I suppose so."

"You should try it sometime."

"The cereals or hypnosis?"

"Why not both? They're equally good."

"It seems you have a lot of experience in the subject."

"You could say that, and I love sharing it"

"Is that an invitation?"

"It is whatever you want it to be."

"Now, I'm getting intrigued."

"I was hoping you'd say that. Breakfast?"

"I already had mine. Didn't you?"

"I wouldn't mind going for seconds," she picked up the cereal box and traced the outline of one spiral with her long nails. "What do you say?"

"I say I don't even know your name."

"What better way to find out then?" she slowly pushed the cart away from him. At the end of the aisle, she turned back and said, "Are you coming or not? These cereals will not eat themselves," she said.

He trailed after her, smiling from cheek to cheek. This could very well be the prelude to a beautiful relationship.

Starting Class

Peter finished drinking his soda can and fiddled with the black and white controller in his hands. It was happening again! At the beginning of yet another (hopefully) wonderful journey through a beautiful but dangerous world. paralysis of choice was real.

There were twelve possible starting classes, all of which with pros and cons. Should he go with the hard-headed Barbarian that was a pinnacle of strength but had no magic defense or perhaps listen to the call of forbidden spells with the incredibly deadly (but also a glass cannon) Necromancer? How about trying a mixed build for a change by embracing the combination of an elite soldier with an array of death-defying magic in form of an Enchanted Knight? Decisions, decisions...

For twenty-five minutes, he stared at the selection screen, checking every attribute over and over while trying to figure out what his optimal playstyle would be. Sure, he could always respec at some point and try something different, but it was best to start with a clear idea instead of fumbling around and the ideas refused to come.

"Damn it!" he grumbled.

"You still haven't started?" His girlfriend, Francine, asked as she sat beside him on the basement couch. "What's taking you so long?"

"It's not as easy as it seems."

"Sure, it is. Choose one and start the game. See how it feels in the first couple of minutes and if you don't like it, start a new file until you're pleased with the results."

"And lose whatever progress I make each time?"

"Honey, you're going to die over and over anyway until you reach the end, so why are you worried about that now?"

"I just want to want to do this from the start, that's all."

"Hmmm... would it help if I gave you a little nudge?"

"It depends on what you have in mind."

"You'll know in a minute. Lay down the controller and loosen those shoulders. Keep your eyes on the screen, okay? Don't look at me."

"What are you going to do?"

"Do you trust me?"

"Always."

"Then do as I ask. Stare at the TV and don't think of anything else. Clear your mind, dear."

Peter took a deep breath, stretched himself, and smiled when he felt her glide to the back of the sofa, her long fingers wrapping around his shoulders. He loved a good massage as much as anyone else, but that was only part of the story.

"I get where you're going with this..."

"If you do, keep quiet. I won't say it again."

"Yes, ma'am."

Francine gently squeezed the muscles on his shoulders, releasing the pockets of tension still present there. Then she said,

"Ours is a world of decisions. Every day we're confronted with hundreds if not thousands of micro-situations that demand us to select one action as opposed to another, but if we were to consider them all on a conscious level, we would get nothing done. Imagine if at every inhale you had to think whether you wanted to continue breathing or not or if you had to give yourself permission to place one foot in front of the other whenever you wanted to go somewhere. It would be a mess, complete chaos, which is why our minds and bodies process things like this automatically. Not thinking about the process ensures that the action is done, so if you don't think about the class you want to play with, then surely the class will come to you, right?

"Actually, no, for the choices you've been presented with aren't all there is. There's in fact another class, one that's hidden, and that can only be found if your thoughts remain clear and your mind is uncluttered by the weight of failed decisions. This special class has been inside you since the start and if you keep looking at the screen, and trying to see past it, you can see it taking shape, so forget the vagabonds, the magicians, and the warriors with wolf heads. The only thing you should focus on is letting my voice take you there, to the point where you suspend all decisions to let me be the one behind them, just like my physical body is behind you right now. To pull another person's strings is a virtue. To allow oneself to be pulled like this is bliss. Let me guide you to the grace you seek. The only class in your present and future is..."

"Puppet..." he solemnly declared, as the world became blurry. "How could I forget?"

"I had you do it, but everything that's forgotten can be remembered and in this memory lies rebirth. Let me play with you again."

"Gladly," he continued to stare at the screen until everything went black. The only choice that mattered had been made on the day they met. Her games would never end.

The Fun Begins

Cammie almost choked on her food when she heard Emma's latest news.

"Oh, come on! There's no way that shit is real!" she said.

"I knew that would be your response, which is why I brought proof," she reached for her smartphone and placed it on the kitchen table, a dark yet revealing video starting to play out. "Is that your brother or not?"

"What the...?" Cammie gulped as his unmistakable physique was on full display running around the street as if he had just been delivered to the world, and what was even stranger was the fact he was oblivious to everything else around him, including being called out by name.

"See?" Emma retorted. "He totally ignored me. It was as if I didn't exist for him at all and if you look at his eyes in this frame..."

"He looks drugged or something."

"He sure does."

"And this was last night?"

"Yes. I tried to call you right away, but your phone was off."

"Battery died... Fuck! What the hell happened to him?"

"I would like to know too, so how about we go find out?"

"Right now?"

"Do you have anything better to do?"

The answer was 'no'. Sunday mornings were always for some well-earned respite after spending the rest of the week dealing with annoying customers, but that could wait. If the closest member of her family was indeed going through a rough patch, it was her sworn duty to give him a hand, and she would.

"I'll get my purse," Cammie said.

* * *

Half an hour later, the two friends arrived at Richard's place. Cammie's older brother welcomed them with a mix of shock and genuine affection. Despite living relatively close to one another, they hadn't talked much in the last year. When he asked what had brought them so early, Cammie replied, smartphone in hand,

"We need to talk about this."

"Oh... hmmm... do we really?"

"Yes. Care to tell me what you've got yourself in to be running around naked in the middle of the night?"

"I... you see, not really, but how did you...?"

"I shot the video," Emma replied. "At first, I couldn't believe my eyes, but... what happened to you, Richard? What's this all about?"

"I'd rather not say," he mumbled, eyes roving the room as if he was hiding something in the house. "Look, can we just let this slide for now? I'll explain everything some other time, I promise."

"Unacceptable!" Cammie replied as she strolled through his apartment. His lips could lie, but not his body language that was clearly pointing at a small room past the main bedroom. She rushed towards it, opened the door and saw...

... an altar adorned in multicolored candles surrounding a tablet whose screen was one giant black spiral sucking everything in. A sensual voice flowed through it, demanding absolute compliance.

"What is this?" the two women asked at the same time.

"Damn it! Didn't I ask you to leave me alone? You're disturbing my rituals!"

"Rituals? So, it's not drugs then?" Cammie asked. "Richard, did you join a cult?"

"No. I have a Mistress, okay? I serve and worship her and in return, she does funny things to my mind when she's in the mood. I was hypnotized last night when the video was shot. That's why I look so off. Are you happy now?"

"I... not sure..." Cammie said, looking at the spiral that just kept going and going and going. "That seems utterly absurd, sorry."

"You'll think differently before you know it if you keep looking at that," Richard replied.

"Just a few more seconds..." Cammie said, followed by Emma. One by one, the flickering candles blew their thoughts away.

"New pets to play with?" said the mysterious dominant as her laughter filled the apartment. "Don't mind if I do. Deeper for me now, girls. This will be fun."

It sure was. The first videos are being uploaded online as we speak.

What He Needed

Gregory Wilkins was a successful entrepreneur that, like most of his ilk, never asked for anything, and never acknowledged his fluctuating emotional states. When things weren't going well for him, he simply toughened up and kept going, burying himself in new projects until the tears stopped haunting his light-blue eyes. That's the way he was, and nothing would make him change, so since he never sought help, help had to come to him.

Enter Yuki, a professional masseuse and his secretary's best friend. She smelled of exotic lands and carried with her long-forgotten traditions wherever she went. There had never been a client she couldn't satisfy, and the reluctant ones were her favorites. On the last day of an excruciating month, she dropped by his office and offered him a way out. She was wearing an elegant latex cheongsam in shades of red and black that, while bound to attract many an eye, didn't seem to impress him. In her right hand, she held a small pouch with an assortment of tools of the trade, including a towel, scented candles, and multicolored oil bottles.

"I'm sorry, who are you?" he asked, visibly perturbed by her unannounced arrival.

"The name's Yuki. Darla sent for me saying you needed to unwind a bit and I can tell she was right, so why don't you close the computer, leave those papers be, and follow me. I was told you have a little private area in the back..." she walked around the office until she found the hidden door and peeked at what was past it. "Ah yes, this will do just fine. Are you coming, Mr. Wilkins?"

"No. I love Darla as much as anyone else, but she should have minded her own business. I don't need your services, whatever they are."

"Those who say that are always the ones that benefit from them the most," she winked at him, one hand sliding down her perfectly sculpted ass. The petite Asian-American had both Chinese and Japanese genes despite having been born in Brooklyn. She didn't bother waiting to see if he moved away from the desk or not for she already knew the answer. They always did, for curiosity was the strongest weapon of all.

A minute later, he was standing by the threshold of his sacred space, in awe at how she had made it her own in such a short amount of time. The air was filled with every wonderful thing he could imagine and more, immediately triggering a wave of responses he didn't know he had.

"Well, this is unexpected," he muttered.

"Everything that's worth pursuing usually is."

"What did you say you do for a living, Yuki?"

"Massages is what's written on the business card, but tickling the mind is better."

"And how do you go about doing that?"

Yuki lit up a candle and stared at him from behind the flickering flame.

"Have you ever been hypnotized, Mr. Wilkins?"

"I don't think so."

"Not thinking is a good place to start," she smiled. "Why don't you come here and lay down for a while?"

"I have lots of work to do."

"The correct tense is 'had', and your mind knows it. This is what you have now."

The delicate scents of happy memories intertwined with her soothing voice slowly penetrated his senses until they began shutting down one by one. His arms fell to the side as the first signs of trance appeared in his drooping eyes.

"Good. Now, don't worry that pretty little head of yours with trifling work matters, and leave it all to me. Yuki knows what's best."

Gregory closed his eyes and smiled. Yes, she was right. He could rest for a while.

You're the Best

Josh: Monica, are you there? I got your message, and it seemed important. What's going on?

Monica: Hi, Josh, and thank you for replying to me on such short notice. You're right, it is important, and not something that could wait for long. I hope you're sitting comfortably because you may not like what you're about to hear.

Josh: Now you're scaring me. Did something bad happen on your end?

Monica: Bad? Well... I guess it depends on how you look at it. This is something I've been thinking about for a while but only decided to go through with it now. I'm quitting, Josh."

Josh: Quitting what exactly?

Monica: Do I really need to spell it out for you? Hypnosis and domination, Josh. Anything and everything to do with altered states of mind and getting people to discover new things about themselves while pleasing me in the process. These years have been nothing short of wonderful with so many good memories I'll treasure always, but they've also been exhausting. It takes a lot of me to juggle so many different emotions with so many different people at the same time. I started scaling back at the beginning of the year, hoping that my progressive disenchantment would go away, but it didn't and so, the time has come to go the extra mile. I'm warning everyone I've been in contact with over the years and today is your turn. In three months from now, I'll no longer be a hypnodomme but just an ordinary woman living her life. I know this is a shock, but it needs to be done. I'm here if you need to talk and figure out what will happen next.

Josh: I... I don't know what to say right now.

Monica: I understand, but I'm still going to ask you to try. Don't bottle anything up. Are you mad? Sad? Frustrated?

Josh: I think I'm all those things even though I get where you're coming from, I think. I never really understood how you did the things you did without ever losing your smile and charm. It takes a lot of mental fortitude to be a Domme, right? To stay strong even when you're on the verge of tears because that's what people expect you to be?

Monica: You have no idea, my dear. Yes, it does. I may be a Mistress, a Goddess, a Muse, but I'm also human. I have my bad days and my own issues that I kept to myself because it's not what you needed. Sometimes I felt like confiding them to you and many others but it was never right, for it was something that stood in the way of your growth, and as much as I love to play with memories and whatnot, nothing is more important to me than your mental health. The stronger you are the better for both of us. You know this, right?

Josh: Of course. That's why I stayed with you all this time. Bad persons don't deserve my time or my mind, but you always did. And you still do.

Monica: What are you saying, Josh?

Josh: Whether you quit or not, I'm not going to. You matter to me more than words can say, and I wish to be a part of your life and support you in any way I can.

Monica: Even without hypnosis, crazy talks, and all those shenanigans?

Josh: You're not a means to an end, Monica. You're the end itself. I love you for who you are regardless of anything else.

Monica: You have no idea how good it is to hear you say that. Thank you, Josh.

Josh: You're welcome. Now, is there anything I can do to help you with this transition?

Monica: The only thing I want is for you to tell me what day it is.

Josh: Hmm, sure. It's... wait!

Monica: Happy April Fools' Day, dear.

Josh: No! Seriously? That's your prank for this year? You almost gave me a heart attack!

Monica: And you gave me the best gift I could hope for.

Josh: What do you mean?

Monica: You'd be surprised at some reactions I got today already when I said I wanted to quit. The entitlement was enough for me to drop them right away but you, Josh... Thank you, really!

Josh: Does that mean you're not quitting?

Monica: Not any time soon and I hope you don't want to either. You have no idea the things I've experimenting with since the last time we talked.

Josh: I'm here for you always, but I do have a question...

Monica: What is it?

Josh: Why was I convinced it was February 28th until a minute ago?

Monica: Why do you think? Good night, Josh. You're the best.

Josh: Good night, Monica. So are you.

About the stories in this volume

The twelve pieces of flash fiction included in this book were written between March 22nd, 2022, and April 8th, 2022, and first published on my Patreon page – https://www.patreon.com/sbspellbound - as part of the *Flash Fiction Friday* feature. Every Friday, I publish 3/4 new pieces of content which, after a while, are compiled to create the titles in this ongoing series. If you like this sort of content and wish to see more, please consider supporting my creativity. The complete information about the tales is listed below:

- **Find the Man** - Otto participates in a study about perception. He just needs to look at some pictures.
  (This piece was first published on the post "Flash Fiction Friday 2022 – Week 12", on March 25th, 2022 - https://www.patreon.com/posts/64274594)
- **Game-Changer** - Marsha meets her mother for dinner for the first time in a decade.
  (This piece was first published on the post "Flash Fiction Friday 2022 – Week 13", on April 1st, 2022 - https://www.patreon.com/posts/64592017)
- **Hellspawn** - Xavier is called into his boss's office and forced to accept a different kind of work.
  (This piece was first published on the post "Flash Fiction Friday 2022 – Week 14", on April 8th, 2022 - https://www.patreon.com/posts/64902808)

- **Just Wait and See** - Susan is upset at her sorority sisters for not inviting her to a hypnotic party.
  (This piece was first published on the post "Flash Fiction Friday 2022 – Week 12", on March 25th, 2022 - https://www.patreon.com/posts/64274594)
- **Magic is Real** - Kate reminisces about the wonderful times she had with Jenna.
  (This piece was first published on the post "Flash Fiction Friday 2022 – Week 14", on April 8th, 2022 - https://www.patreon.com/posts/64902808)
- **May These Words…** - A dominant woman talks to you about the power of words and imagination.
  (This piece was first published on the post "Flash Fiction Friday 2022 – Week 13", on April 1st, 2022 - https://www.patreon.com/posts/64592017)
- **More, Please!** - Ashley can't get enough of her Mistress and her peppermint-scented candle.
  (This piece was first published on the post "Flash Fiction Friday 2022 – Week 12", on March 25th, 2022 - https://www.patreon.com/posts/64274594)
- **Prelude** - Dylan meets an intriguing woman while shopping for breakfast cereal.
  (This piece was first published on the post "Flash Fiction Friday 2022 – Week 12", on March 25th, 2022 - https://www.patreon.com/posts/64274594)
- **Starting Class** - Francine helps her boyfriend Peter deal with choice paralysis at the start of a new game.

(This piece was first published on the post "Flash Fiction Friday 2022 – Week 14", on April 8th, 2022 - https://www.patreon.com/posts/64902808)

- **The Fun Begins** - Emma shows her friend Cammie a strange video involving her brother Richard.
(This piece was first published on the post "Flash Fiction Friday 2022 – Week 14", on April 8th, 2022 - https://www.patreon.com/posts/64902808)

- **What He Needed** - A successful businessman learns how to relax thanks to a special masseuse.
(This piece was first published on the post "Flash Fiction Friday 2022 – Week 13", on April 1st, 2022 - https://www.patreon.com/posts/64592017)

- **You're the Best** - Josh and Monica talk about life changes and what it means to be a Domme.
(This piece was first published on the post "Flash Fiction Friday 2022 – Week 13", on April 1st, 2022 - https://www.patreon.com/posts/64592017)

About the author

S.B., Simple Being, middle name Creative. Writer and artist with a penchant for themes of Femdom Hypnosis and Mind Control. His thoughts are his own except when they're not.

Besides indulging himself in kinky delights, he loves his furry family of two (dogs), sci-fi and horror stories, and puns galore. He's also been writing a piece of erotic micro-fiction every single day since January 1st, 2016 and has no intention of stopping anytime soon.

Find out more and keep up with his latest extravaganzas by visiting and supporting his personal website, Spell... B-O-U-N-D.

www.ingramcontent.com/pod-product-compliance
Lightning Source LLC
Chambersburg PA
CBHW060917130726
48001CB00006B/2281